Good night

Catherine and Laurence Anholt

Playing games since early morning.

Now we're tired, baby's yawning.

Muddy clothes all in a heap.

Bubbly water, warm and deep.

Rub-a-dub and wriggle jiggle.

Tickly tummy, giggle giggle.

Brush your teeth to keep them white.

Help me get my buttons right.

Much too tired to walk myself.

Choose a story from the shelf.

Jumping, bouncing in the air.

A picture book for us to share.

Give a kiss and say 'Good night'.

One last cuddle, squeeze me tight.

Close your eyes. No more peeping.